This
Beauty and the Beast
ANNUAL 2018
belongs to:

Maia

Lyall

EGMONT
We bring stories to life

First published in Great Britain in 2017 by Egmont UK Limited
The Yellow Building, 1 Nicholas Road, London W11 4AN

Content written and adapted by Catherine Shoolbred
Designed by Jeannette O'Toole

© 2017 Disney Enterprises, Inc.

ISBN 978 1 4052 8860 6
68226/1

Printed in Italy

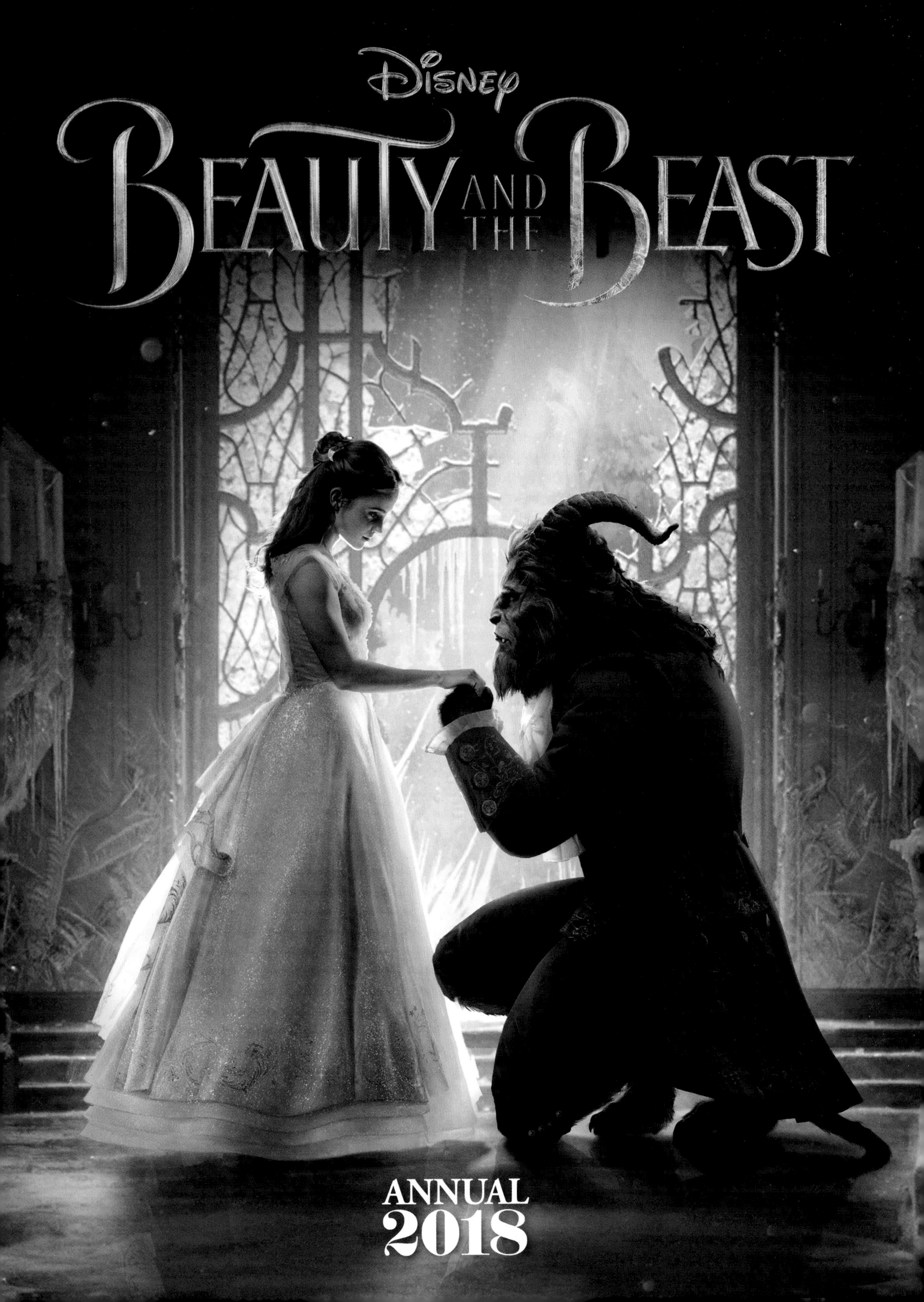
Disney
Beauty and the Beast
ANNUAL
2018

CONTENTS

GET TO KNOW ... *Belle*

- *Belle* is SMART and **kind** to others.

- *Belle* longs to leave her village and have an ADVENTURE.

- She isn't AFRAID to be **different.**

- She LOVES stories, BOOKS, reading and **learning.**

- *Belle* looks past appearances and sees the good in others, like the **Beast.**

GET TO KNOW ... THE *Beast*

- The **Beast** is a prince under an ENCHANTMENT.

- He and his CASTLE are put under a **spell** after he selfishly refuses to help an Enchantress in disguise.

- He guards the enchanted rose. To break the **spell**, he must learn to LOVE and be LOVED in return.

- The **Beast** gives *Belle* his library when he learns that she **loves books.**

- The **Beast** has a **bad temper**, but *Belle* helps teach him to be a BETTER MAN.

DOODLE STORY MAGIC

Belle enjoys
reading *exciting*
stories.

Draw what
you think she
is *reading*
about.

- Maurice is *Belle's* father.

- He is an **inventor** and makes beautiful music boxes.

- Whenever he travels he brings home a rose for *Belle*.

- He travels to markets with his horse, **Philippe**, to sell his music boxes.

- *Belle* knows Maurice is in trouble when Philippe returns home without him.

GET TO KNOW ... *Gaston*

- Gaston is handsome, vain and **arrogant**.

- He has a **cruel heart** and loves hunting.

- He is **boastful** and has lots of admirers in the village.

- LeFou is his best friend. He will do anything for Gaston.

- Gaston wants *Belle* to **marry** him. He would do anything to make it happen, even attack a **Beast.**

WORDSEARCH

Search the puzzle for the words listed below.
Circle the ones you find!

BELLE, PHILIPPE, GASTON, GARDEROBE, BEAST, COGSWORTH, LUMIERE, CHIP, PLUMETTE, CHAPEAU, LEFOU, ROSA, ENCHANTED, MAURICE, CASTLE,

```
K E E R I R W Q E L O E G K R
C N T L O V T A O V H T A S H
L C I S T A K L M B T T R W Q
N H E J Y S T M V R R E D F K
L A D I T V A A R Y O M E Q B
H N L E F O U C W M W U R C E
T T E R E I M U L G S L O H L
P E U S V P V V C H G P B A L
Q D P H I L I P P E O B E P E
Y L E J F E R J Y Y C U D E V
G I E Y H E X Y U L E E G A B
U B G A S T O N F O B Y P U E
L I W B O T M A U R I C E E A
L U I F M C H I P L E M N E S
R Y K X N P Y X C K F J D E T
```

Answers on page 68.

BELLE'S LIBRARY

Belle loves to read. Books take her on new adventures. Do you like reading too? Add drawings in the spaces below to show a fairy tale, an adventure story and a comedy.

FAIRY TALES

When Belle reads fairy tales, she enters fantastical worlds where even the impossible can happen.

COMEDIES

Comedies can always make Belle laugh with their wit and humour.

ADVENTURE TALES

In adventure stories, Belle gets to go on journeys alongside her favourite characters.

GET TO KNOW ...
THE *Enchanted Servants*

Lumiere is a happy-go-lucky castle footman. He lights up the room with his candles and cheerful personality.

Plumette, the maid turned feather duster, is Lumiere's girlfriend.

Cogsworth is in charge of the castle. He is very loyal to the Beast, his master, and hopes that he'll find true love and break the spell.

Mrs. Potts is the castle governess and Chip's mother. She knows that a cup of tea can fix most problems.

Chip is friendly and energetic. He loves racing around the castle exploring.

Chapeau is the helpful hat stand in the castle.

Madame de Garderobe is a magical wardrobe. She's very excited to dress Belle.

17

Beauty and the Beast

There once lived a handsome but selfish Prince. His life was full of wealth and parties until the night he refused shelter to a BEGGAR WOMAN.

The BEGGAR WOMAN was an enchantress in disguise. When the Prince refused to look beyond appearances, she revealed herself as an enchantress and punished the Prince by turning him into a Beast.

The Prince would stay a Beast until he found someone who, unlike him, could look beyond appearances. But if the last petal fell off the enchanted rose before then, he would remain a beast FOREVER!

In a nearby village, a kind girl called Belle dreamed of having adventures like those in her BOOKS.

Gaston was a vain and arrogant man. His friend, LeFou, praised him and did anything he wanted. Gaston was determined to marry Belle even thought she wanted nothing to do with him.

Belle's father Maurice made beautiful music boxes. As he finished his latest one, he packed up his cart and Philippe, his horse, and set off to the market.

Gaston asked Belle to marry him again. She again said no, she wanted more than Gaston and the village. She wanted an adventure!

Meanwhile, Maurice got lost in the woods. He and his horse, Philippe, were chased by wolves. He sought shelter in the grounds of a hidden castle.

THE STORY CONTINUES ON PAGE 28

WORD SCRAMBLE

Can you unscramble the letters to spell the characters' names?

L B L E E

1   B E L L E

M E U I E R L

2   L U M I E R E

O T H G C O W S R

3   C O G S W O R T H

S M R S T O P T

4   M R S P O T T S

B E R A G D E O R

5

N A G T O S

6   G A S T O N

Answers on page 68.

22

SILHOUETTES

Whose silhouettes are these? Draw lines to match
them to the right characters below.

A

B

C

D

1

2

3

4

Answers on page 68.

23

DOODLE BELLE'S BOOKS

Belle spends lots of time in the library.
Decorate all her books.

ADD IT UP!

Can you solve these sums?
Write the answer in the box at the end of each row.

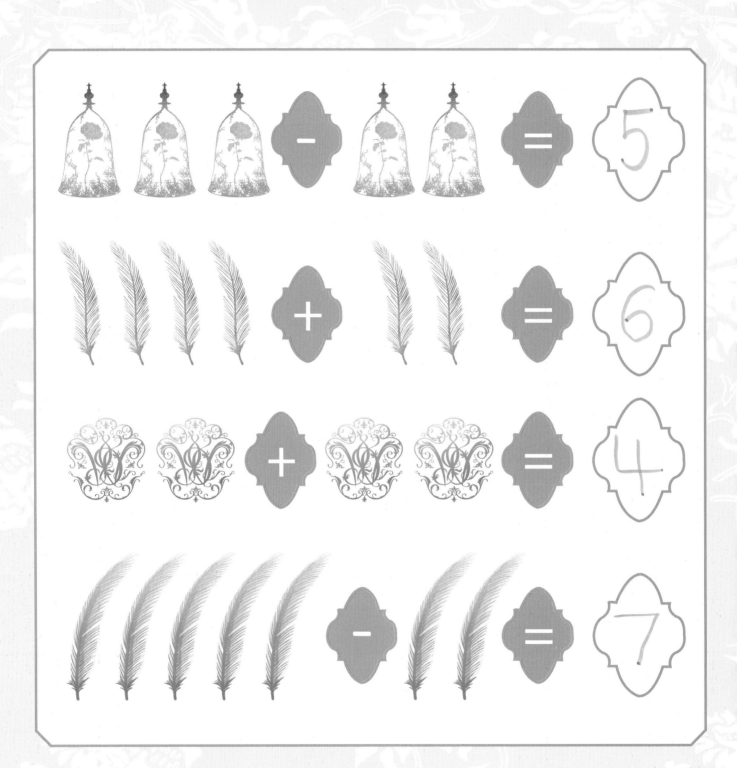

Answers on page 68.

ENCHANTING PATTERNS

Look at each line and figure out the missing object.
Can you complete the patterns?

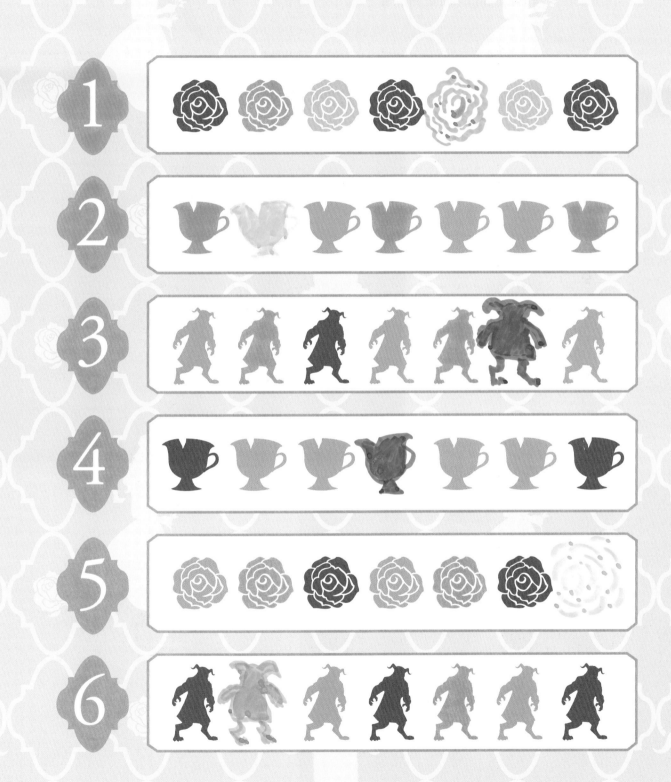

Answers on page 68.

The furniture in the magical castle was alive! When Maurice sat at the dining table, Chip, a cup, spoke to him. Frightened, Maurice ran away.

But as Maurice left, he saw a white rose that he was sure Belle would love. When he picked it, the Beast, who owned the castle, took him prisoner.

When Maurice's horse, Philippe, returned from the market without him, Belle knew he was in trouble. Philippe took Belle back to the castle.

Belle found Maurice in a cell. He told her to flee, but then the Beast appeared. Belle felt responsible, because her father had picked the rose for her.

Belle pretended to say goodbye to her father, but instead pushed him out of the cell so she would be the prisoner instead. Maurice was thrown out of the castle and went to get help.

Suddenly Lumiere, a candelabra, and Cogsworth, a mantle clock, spoke to Belle. They took her to a bedroom where Madame de Garderobe, a magical wardrobe, dressed her up.

In the village, Gaston still wanted to marry Belle. When Maurice told everyone about the Beast, Gaston didn't believe him, but he said he'd rescue Belle thinking she'd then have to marry him.

Belle made friends with the enchanted servants in the castle. Mrs. Potts, the teapot, told her that the Beast was not as terrible as he appeared. Belle explored the West Wing, which was forbidden.

THE STORY CONTINUES ON PAGE 40

PUZZLING PATHS

Chip can't wait to meet up with Belle, the Beast and Lumiere.
Follow the paths to see which one leads to each friend.

Belle

Lumiere

The Beast

A

B

C

Answers on page 68.

COLOURFUL BELLE

Trace over the letters to reveal the colours of Belle's rose and dress.
Then colour the paint splodges to match.

red

yellow

FILL IN THE PHRASE

Can you figure out the phrase below?
Write the letters in the boxes.

S	N	T	C	H

A	D	R	O	E

E	N	C	H	A	N	T	E	D

R	O	S	E

Answers on page 68.

CUT ALONG HERE

CUT ALONG HERE

WHO SAID WHAT?

Belle, the Beast, Lumiere, Gaston, Cogsworth and Mrs. Potts say the below phrases. But who said what? Draw lines to match each character to what they said.

1. "Be our guest."

2. "Don't spill tea. Or secrets."

3. "It's hero time."

4. "Forever can spare a minute."

5. "I love being a clock."

6. "You will join me for dinner."

A

B

C

D

E

F

Answers on page 68.

Belle found an enchanted rose in the Beast's room. The Beast was angry, because he thought she might harm it. Frightened, Belle escaped from the castle on Philippe.

But wolves surrounded Belle and Philippe. The Beast saved them, but he was badly wounded by the wolves. Grateful for his help, Belle helped him home.

Maurice, Gaston and LeFou had been searching for the Beast's castle for ages. Maurice realised Gaston was mean and selfish so he said he'd never marry Belle. Gaston tied up Maurice and left him in the woods.

As Belle looked after the Beast, Mrs. Potts told her the Beast's story. Belle wanted to help him and the enchanted servants. Belle read books to the Beast and they shared their love of reading.

Belle and the Beast got to know and like each other. Maurice escaped from the woods, but the villagers didn't believe him about the Beast or that Gaston had left him. Maurice was to be locked up.

In the castle, Belle had a wonderful evening dancing with the Beast. But she missed her father and when the Beast gave her a magic mirror to look at him, she saw that her father needed her help.

The last petal of the magic rose was about to fall, but the Beast let Belle go to her father. To prove that he was telling the truth, she showed Gaston the Beast in the mirror. Gaston convinced the villagers to destroy the Beast!

The enchanted servants fought back against the villagers who ran away. Gaston was determined to kill the Beast. Belle broke his arrows, but he shot the Beast before the footbridge he was standing on crumbled and he fell to his doom.

THE STORY CONTINUES ON PAGE 50

DREAM DRESS

Doesn't Belle's dress look beautiful?
Design your own dress and pretty shoes to match.

TALE AS OLD AS TIME

Draw lines to match each phrase to the right character.

1 Ready to chip in

2 Swept up in excitement

3 Ticktock

4 Never enough closet space

5 Light the way

6 The one who must break the spell

A

B

C

D

E

F

Answers on page 68.

SUDOKU

Can you fill in the gaps to complete each sudoku puzzle?

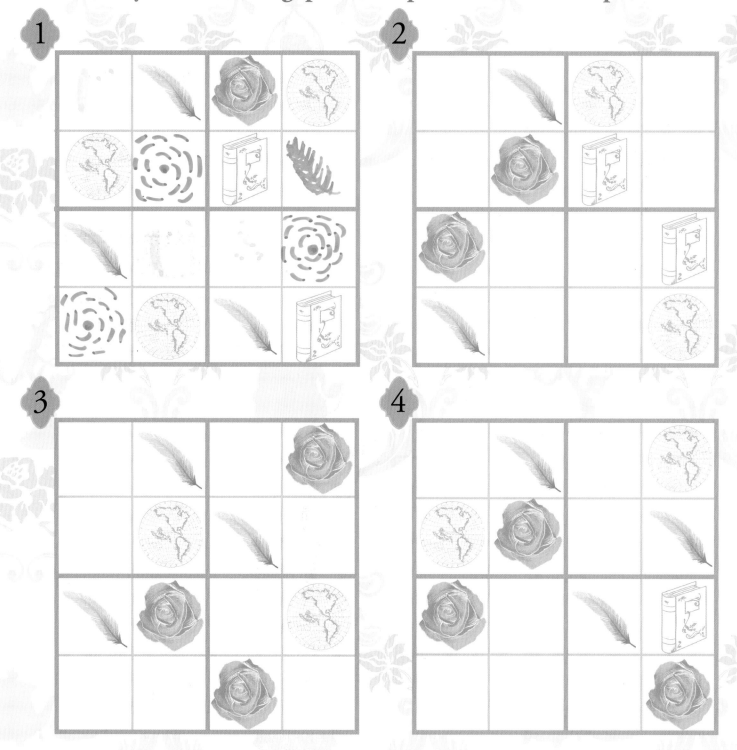

TIP: no item can appear more than once in any row or column.

Answers on page 68.

WORD SCRAMBLE

Can you unscramble the letters
to spell the characters' names?

T L E M U E P T

1 PLUMETTE

E U F O L

2 LEFOU

A I U M E R C

3 MAURICE

I H P C

4 CHIP

S E B T A

5 BEAST

A C P E A H U

6 CHAPEAU

Answers on page 68.

47

DOODLE BELLE'S DRESS

Roses are Belle's *favourite* flower.

Draw a *rose-covered* dress for Belle.

In tears, Belle rushed to the Beast. She had shared so much with him and she now knew his kind and kindred soul. She was horrified to see the Beast take his final breath.

As the last petal of the enchanted rose fell, the castle's curse started to take effect. Cogsworth, Lumiere and the rest of the enchanted servants turned into lifeless objects.

As Belle kissed the Beast saying, "I love you," the Beast's body rose into the air and he turned back into a human. Shocked but thrilled, Belle and her Prince kissed.

Throughout the castle, the curse was lifted. The cold grey castle walls became a warm gold and the ice and snow became bright green grass.

Lumiere's candles turned back into arms and Cogsworth's clock hands become a moustache. Mrs. Potts, Chip and the rest of the staff celebrated as they all became human again.

Belle and the Prince held a ball to celebrate. Surrounded by family old and new, Belle had never been happier. Her tale ended as all tales should ... happily ever after.

The End

QUESTIONS ABOUT THE STORY

How well do you remember the story?
See how quickly you can answer these questions about it.

1

Who put a spell on the Prince?

 Gaston

 an enchantress
(dressed as a beggar)

2

What did the enchantress give the Beast?

 an enchanted tulip

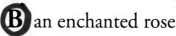 an enchanted rose

3

What did Belle dream of?

 having an adventure

 staying in the village

4

What does Maurice do for a living?

 he makes music boxes

he's a farmer

5

When Maurice gets lost, what chases him?

 chickens

 wolves

6

When he's under the spell what is Lumiere?

 a candelabra

 a coat rack

7

What is Mrs. Potts' son called?

 Cup

 Chip

8

What did Belle say that broke the curse?

 I love you

 Goodbye

Answers on page 68.

MARVELLOUS MESSAGE

Trace over the dotted letters to find out what Belle's message is.

HELLO, IS ANYONE THERE?

Answers on page 68.

SUDOKU

Can you fill in the gaps to complete each puzzle?

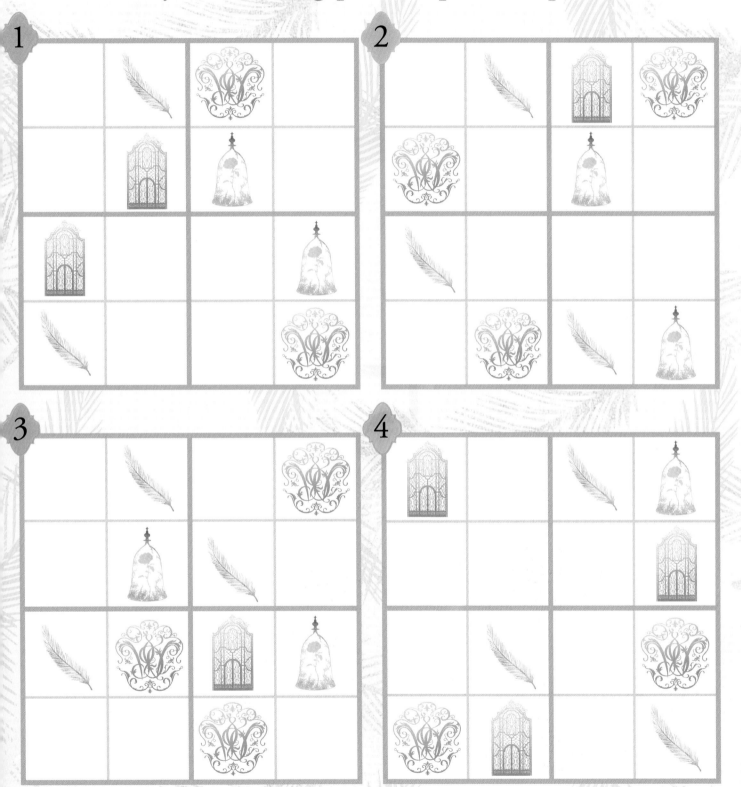

TIP: no item can appear more than once in any row or column.

Answers on page 68.

ADD IT UP!

Can you solve these sums?
Add numbers in the boxes to complete them.

$$2 + 4 = $$

$$2 + 5 = 7$$

$$3 + 5 = 8$$

Answers on page 68.

ROSE TRAIL

Follow the trail. How many roses are there?
Write the number in the box below.

7

Answers on page 68.

WHEELY GOOD FUN

Follow the word wheel to find Beauty and the
Beast characters. Write their names below.

1 BELLE   2 BEAST

3 CHIP   4 GASTON

Answers on page 68.

COUNT THEM UP
How many of each object can you count?

1 — 6
2 — 8
3 — 3
4 — 4
5 — 2
6 — 1

Answers on page 68.

FILL IN THE PHRASE

Can you figure out the phrase below? Use the key to write the letters in the boxes.

T B A S Y I U O

E N D W H F

BEAUTY IS

FOUND WITHIN

Answers on page 68.

FOLLOW THE LINES

Everyone is looking for Mrs. Potts.
Follow the lines to see who is going to find her.

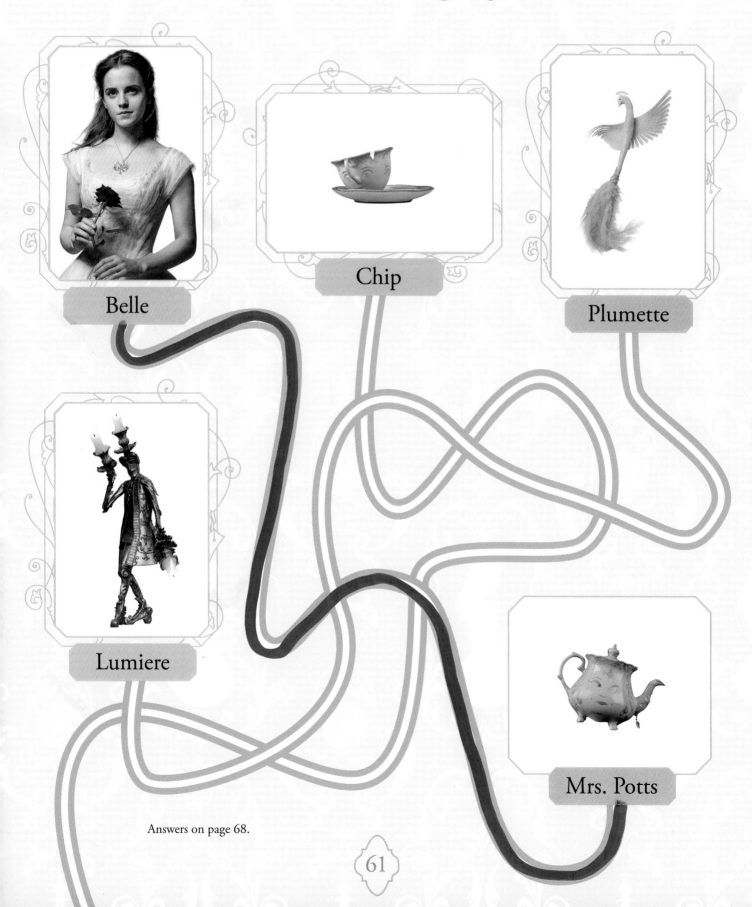

Belle

Chip

Plumette

Lumiere

Mrs. Potts

Answers on page 68.

QUIZ TIME!

How well do you know Belle and the Beast?
Tick the correct picture to answer each question.

1 Who is under a **magic spell?**

2 Whose father is **Maurice?**

3 Who is a **royal in disguise?**

4 Who has an **enchanted rose?**

5 Who wants an **adventure?**

6 Who has a **bad temper?**

Answers on page 68.

COMPLETE THE PATTERN

Look at each line and figure out the missing object.
Can you complete the patterns?

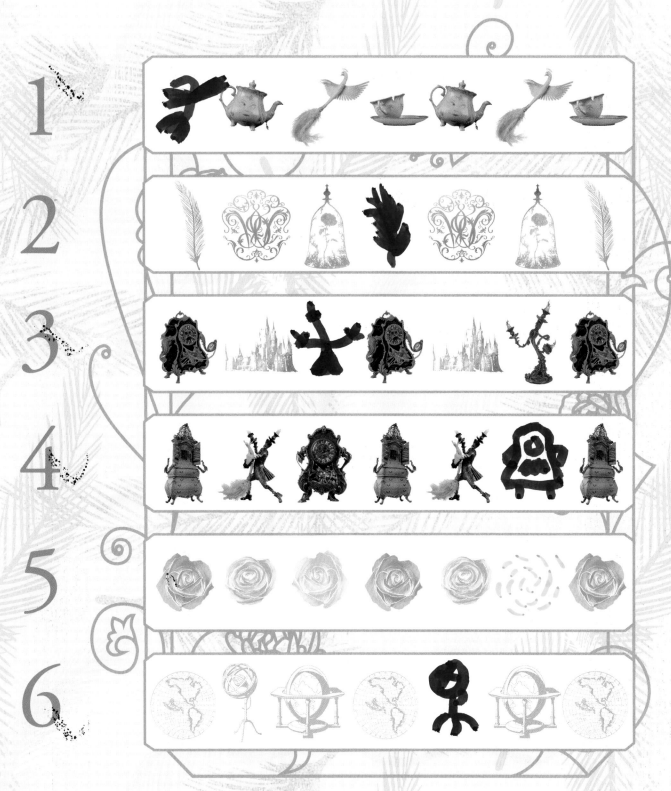

Answers on page 68.

MAZE

Can you get Belle and her friends to the enchanted castle?
Help each of them find a way through the maze.

START

START

START

FINISH

Answers on page 68.

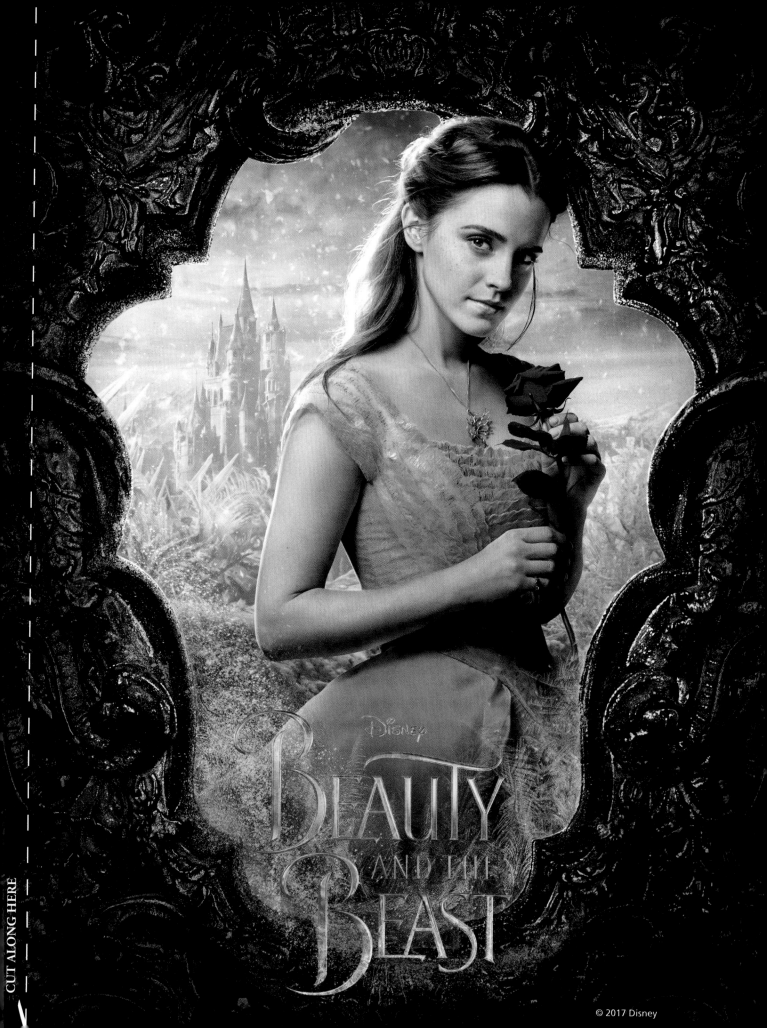

Disney
BEAUTY
AND THE
BEAST

WHO SAID WHAT?

Belle, Gaston, Cogsworth, Lumiere, the Beast and Mrs. Potts say the below phrases. But who said what? Draw lines to match the character to what they said.

1 "Do you think I'm odd?"

2 "At your service."

3 "Cup of tea, dear?"

4 "This is the day your dreams come true."

5 "Not what I appear."

6 "What time is it?"

A

B

C

D

E

F

Answers on page 68.

ANSWERS

PAGE 14 WORDSEARCH

PAGE 22 WORD SCRAMBLE
1. BELLE
2. LUMIERE
3. COGSWORTH
4. MRS POTTS
5. GARDEROBE
6. GASTON

PAGE 23 SILHOUETTES
A – 2, B – 3, C – 4, D – 1.

PAGE 26 ADD IT UP!
3 – 2 = 1, 4 + 2 = 6,
2 + 2 = 4, 5 – 2 = 3.

PAGE 27 ENCHANTING PATTERNS

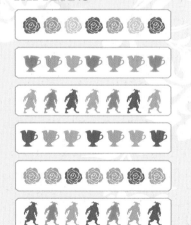

PAGE 32 PUZZLING PATHS
PATH A = LUMIERE
PATH B = THE BEAST
PATH C = BELLE

PAGE 34 FILL IN THE PHRASE
ENCHANTED ROSE

PAGE 39 WHO SAID WHAT?
1 – C, 2 – D, 3 –E, 4 – A,
5 – B, 6 – F.

PAGE 45 TALE AS OLD AS TIME
1 – E, 2 – D, 3 –B, 4 – F,
5 – C, 6 – A.

PAGE 46 SUDOKU

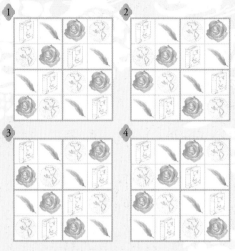

PAGE 47 WORD SCRAMBLE
1. PLUMETTE   2. LEFOU
3. MAURICE   4. CHIP
5. BEAST   6. CHAPEAU

PAGE 53 QUESTIONS ABOUT THE STORY
1. B, 2. B, 3. A, 4. A, 5. B,
6. A, 7. B, 8. A.

PAGE 54 MARVELLOUS MESSAGE
HELLO, IS ANYONE THERE?

PAGE 55 SUDOKU

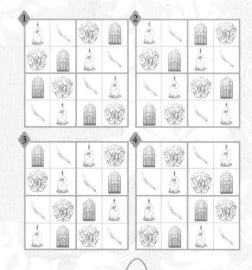

PAGE 56 ADD IT UP!
2 + 4 = 6, 2 + 5 = 7, 3 + 5 = 8.

PAGE 57 ROSE TRAIL
8 ROSES.

PAGE 58 WHEELY GOOD FUN
1. BELLE 2. BEAST
3. CHIP 4. GASTON

PAGE 59 COUNT THEM UP
1. 6, 2. 8, 3. 3, 4. 4, 5. 2, 6. 1.

PAGE 60 FILL IN THE PHRASE
BEAUTY IS FOUND WITHIN

PAGE 61 FOLLOW THE LINES
BELLE FINDS MRS. POTTS.

PAGE 62 QUIZ TIME!
1. BEAST   2. BELLE
3. BEAST   4. BEAST
5. BELLE   6. BEAST

PAGE 63 COMPLETE THE PATTERN

PAGE 64 MAZE

PAGE 67 WHO SAID WHAT?
1 – A, 2 – C, 3 – D, 4 – E,
5 – F, 6 – B.

Beauty Is Found Within